HOPE for Someday

by Vincent Ewald
Illustrated by Tom Leigh

The Ark Animal Shelter • Cherryfield, Maine • thearkpets.org

All stories, like wandering streams
and moonlit dreams, have their beginnings.
Our story begins on a cold, still night,
in front of an old rundown store, in the middle
of somewhere not too far away.

"Pipp. Pipp. Are you awake?" asked a shivering little voice, tucked away in a straw basket, curled up in a ragged, musty wool blanket. "I'm too cold to sleep," replied Pippy.

"Is somebody going to come for us?"
asked Poppy.
"Soon," said Pippy, gazing out
at the half moon sky.
"Where will they take us?
Poppy added.
"Somewhere safe, now rest
yourself," encouraged Pippy.

Poppy buried herself a little further
into the blanket, nudging her cold nose
under Pippy's smooth belly.
"Will we ever have
our own home, Pipp?" asked Poppy.

"Someday," said Pippy. "Someday."

Off in the distance, Pippy heard
the sound of approaching footsteps
crunching over the frosty ground,
making their way closer and closer
to their basket. "Someone's coming,"
Poppy said excitedly. "Is it mom?"
Pippy peeked over the rim of the basket.
"No, I think it's a big person."

"Well, well, what do we have here?" said a woman in a soft, kind voice as she peeled back the musty blanket, unveiling the two lonely pups.

"We'll get you to the shelter first thing tomorrow," said the woman, stroking Poppy's soft little ears. "But you," she said holding Pippy in her arms like a newborn baby, "are going to stay with me."

So now our story takes a sudden twist in the road as Pippy and Poppy find themselves carried away to somewhere altogether new.

Much to their liking, they soon found themselves in the warmth of the kind woman's kitchen. They were fed, given a fresh blanket to lie on, and sung to sleep beside the glow of a cracklin' wood stove.

When Pippy awoke the next morning, Poppy
was already on her way to the local shelter.
So instead of Poppy curled by his side,
he found himself alongside a shaggy,
and rather tall, curious cat named Forrest.

What's your story, kid?" asked Forrest as he circled around the confused pup. "My story? Well, I don't really know, see we were..."

Forrest quickly interrupted Pippy and drew his attention across the room.

"OK, listen up and listen good.
See that cat over there, that's Caster.
He thinks he runs the place, and he don't
like newcomers. So watch your tail, kid,"
advised Forrest.

As you can imagine, Pippy was very confused, very tired, and very much wondering where Poppy was. But he was also excited to explore his new surroundings.

Caster, the big black cat in question, quietly watched Pippy from on top of the kitchen counter, but with his eyes almost closed as if he weren't really interested at all.

Pippy soon sniffed out something in a can
on the floor. It was smelly, but it sure
seemed like food. Before he could take a bite,
he looked up and saw Caster glaring down
at him with wide, angry eyes.

With a lightening flash, everything went bright,
and then dark, as Caster took a swipe at Pippy's
right eye. Forrest jumped in and knocked
Caster off his paws, but it was too late.

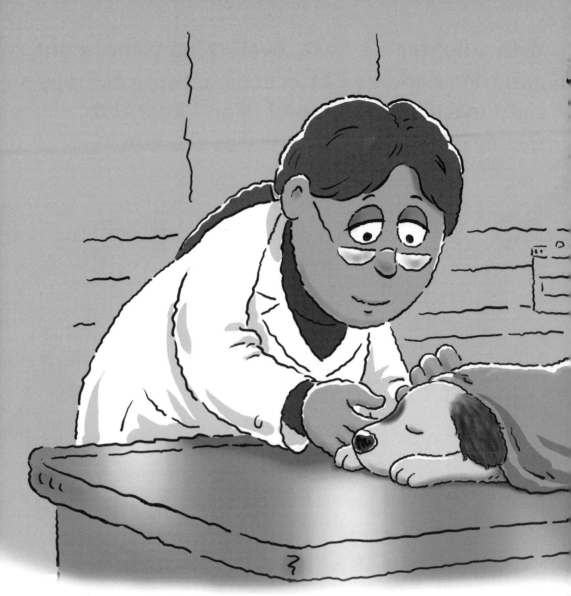

Pippy closed his eyes in pain, listening
to the sound of cats battling it out.
The kitchen door swung open and the kind
woman chased the screaming cats away,
wrapped Pippy in a towel and quickly
carrried him off.

She realized her home was not the best place for the young pup after all, so he was now in the hands of a local veterinarian getting the blow from Caster fixed up. Pippy would soon find himself swept away to yet another place, altogether strange and new.

After what seemed like days of dizzying sights and sounds, Pippy at last heard something familiar, Poppy's sweet, comforting voice. "Pipp. Pipp. Are you awake?" asked Poppy with worried excitement.

"I think so," said Pippy. "Where are we now?"
"The animal shelter," replied Poppy, carefully
examining Pippy's puffy white eye patch.
"What happened to your eye?" asked Poppy.
"Caster the big black cat got me," he answered
in a low, gloomy voice.

"You don't have to worry now,"
Poppy uttered with confidence.
"They take good care of you here, Pipp.
They feed you yummy food and scratch you
in all the right spots. I just had my first bath.
Look at my shiny new coat."

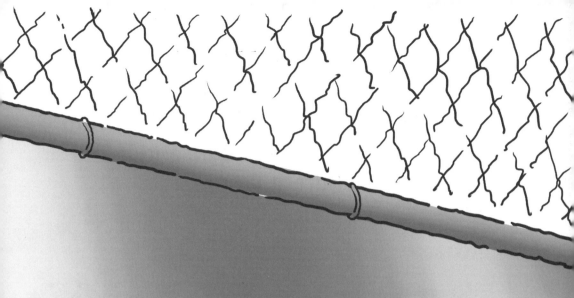

"It's a little hard at the moment," said Pippy, resting his weary head upon his paw. "Right," replied Poppy. "Well, cheer up Pipp, they'll have you as good as new in no time."

Poppy was right. Pippy did cheer up, and his eye healed up too. Life would always be a bit blurry though that eye, but he could make things out well enough, and it certainly didn't hurt anymore.

Each day at the shelter was much like the next for the two pups. They got lots of love and attention from all the caring shelter people, who fed them twice a day, showed them how to go potty outdoors and even taught them how to walk on a rope called a leash.

Pippy and Poppy liked playing together in their special place called a pen, tugging at toys and chasing balls around.

This was the best life they knew.

Sometimes, people they had never seen before would visit and spend time petting and playing with them. They'd take them for walks, give them treats and scratch them in all the right spots. That was always an exciting day!

In the pen right next to Pippy and Poppy
was a wise older Shepherd named Sullivan.
The shelter people took very good care
of Sullivan too. Strangers would also come
and take him for walks, play ball with him
and scratch him in all the right spots.

Sullivan whispered over to Pippy...
"Hey Pup, this is my last day at the shelter.
I'm going home today. Don't worry,
we'll see you out there."

Pippy and Poppy
looked up at Sullivan. He
stood proud and tall, gazing out
the sunlit windows with all the hope
and excitement that a day in the life
of a shelter animal could bring.

"Will we ever have our own home?"
Poppy asked Pippy as they too gazed
out the sunlit windows with all the hope
and wonder that a day in the life
of a shelter animal could bring.

"Someday," said Pipp. "Someday."

Will Pippy and Poppy find their forever home?
Stay tuned for their next adventure,
Home Is Forever.

Thank you to all the wonderful people who contributed to the completion of this book, and a special thanks for the grant support from The Maine Community Foundation, who works with donors and partners to improve the quality of life for all Maine people.

Where you can find a friend for life

The Ark is a no-kill animal shelter located in Cherryfield, in beautiful DownEast Maine. Founded in 1984, The Ark is committed to providing compassionate care and placement of homeless animals through the shelter operation, spaying and neutering pets to alleviate overpopulation, and promoting and improving the welfare of all animals through community outreach and education.

The Ark Animal Shelter
60 Barber Lane, PO Box 276
Cherryfield, ME 04622
207-546-3484 • thearkpets.org